Copyright ©2024 Tammy Savitts Chaisson

Written and Illustrated by Tammy Savitts Chaisson

Photograph of Tammy Savitts Chaisson by Michael Messing Photography

Published by Miriam Laundry Publishing Company
miriamlaundry.com

All rights reserved. This book or any portion thereof may not be reproduced or used in any manner whatsoever without the express written permission from the author except for the use of brief quotations in a book review.

HC ISBN 978-1-77944-147-8
PB ISBN 978-1-77944-146-1
e-Book ISBN 978-1-77944-145-4

FIRST EDITION

# Santa's Nice List

This book would not be possible without my supporters, the first being my husband, Frank, who encouraged me DAILY and read every change without complaint. He is my DREAM MAKER.

My family: sisters Janet Pertuit, Peggy Boudreaux, Mitzi Wright, niece Sandra Daras, mother-in-law Enola Chaisson, sister and brother-in-law Susan and John Pennington and my friend Kary Irle, who probably hated to open her email to find another draft to read, but she graciously did.

My Sunday morning coffee drinkers and texting friends, Cody Adams, Patricia Tucker and Cindy Lagarde, who gave an honest opinion when I needed one.

I knew that if I ever wrote a book, I wanted to illustrate it. Emily LaJaunie is a local graphic designer who helped me with the whole process from beginning to end. She was a life saver!

I can't forget who woke me up early EVERY morning to start writing this book— they are my hungry cats. They would meow in my face and paw at my pajamas until I woke up.

My last thank you is to the many cups of dark roast coffee, which kept me focused after all those early morning awakenings.

Mommy rushed into my bedroom. "Wake up, Allie!"

Why was Mommy so excited?
Then I remembered.
"We're going to see Santa!"

I ran to wake up my little brother, Bobby.
"We're going to see Santa today, Bobby!"

Mommy asked me to watch Bobby while she cooked breakfast. I didn't mind watching my little brother. He listened to me, because I was his big sister.

"Do you want to draw a picture for Santa? I have lots of crayons." I added, "I'll draw one with you." *Mine will be really pretty*, I thought.

"This will make Santa happy," I explained to Bobby. "He'll give us what we want for Christmas."

"Breakfast is ready!" Mommy shouted.

We ran to the kitchen. "Look what I did, Mommy," Bobby giggled.

Bobby and I held up our drawings.

"I love your pictures," Mommy said. "And Santa will too!"

We finally made it to the car. We were on our way to see Santa! Bobby fell asleep right away, but I was too excited to sleep. How could Bobby sleep with me and Mommy singing Christmas songs the whole way?!

There were many people in the store where Santa was visiting.

Mommy told us to hold hands so we would not get lost.

"Oh my," Mommy sighed. "Santa's line is long. Will you two kids be good waiting?"

We jumped up and down and screamed, "Yes! Yes!"

We could hear other kids crying. Some kids were even running in and out of line!

Bobby and I were good as we moved towards Santa.
We told each other what presents we wanted him to
bring us on Christmas Day.

When Bobby squirmed a bit, I whispered a warning. "We have to be good all the time. We never know when Santa is watching us."

As we got closer, Mommy asked, "Can you see Santa yet?"

There were lots of taller kids in front of me,
so I stepped out of line to look.

I finally saw Santa. He looked so scary. I couldn't move!
I was afraid—afraid of Santa! But why was I afraid of him?

Maybe it was because his eyebrows looked like two white, hairy caterpillars dancing with each other every time he laughed!

Or maybe it was because there might be thousands of tiny spiders inside his beard!

What if I sat on Santa's lap and the spiders jumped out and crawled on me?

What if I got caught in his beard and couldn't get out?

I wanted to go home!

I got back in line and looked at Bobby.
He could see Santa now, and he was smiling.
How could he be happy and not afraid? Maybe he wasn't smiling at Santa, but at someone else.

"Are you looking at Santa?" I asked him.

He nodded his head yes.

"Do you want to leave?"

He shook his head no.

I wanted to get out of Santa's line, but I didn't want anyone to know I was afraid.

"Don't you think his beard is weird?
Don't you think his eyebrows are scary?"

"No."

"But you can hardly see his eyes and mouth," I said.
"It's okay if you don't want to sit on Santa's lap."

Bobby pouted. "I want Santa!"

I tried again. "We can go home. We don't need to ask him for our presents."

Bobby looked like he might cry.

"Please, Bobby? Mommy or Daddy can write letters to Santa for us."

Then Bobby did start to cry.

Oh, no! We were next! Santa's beard looked really weird this close up. I did not want to cry! *It's just hair. It's just hair,* I kept telling myself.

Suddenly, I knew what to do—I'd let Bobby go first! Then I'd pretend I was too old for Santa.

Santa called us up.

"Go on, Bobby," I told him. "I'll wait for you."

But Bobby tugged on my hand. *Hmmm, I thought. If I hold Bobby's hand, Mommy will think it's Bobby who is afraid.*

Santa reached down and helped us sit on his knees.

His beard touched me! It was soft on my cheek.

Santa smelled like Mommy's homemade cookies.

I didn't see any dancing caterpillars, or a single spider in his beard!

Santa made us laugh, and he told us we were sweet.
"I know you've both been good this year," he said.

I had the biggest smile on my face when our picture was taken.

Before jumping off his soft lap, we gave Santa our drawings. In return, he gave each of us a candy cane. "Thank you! Thank you, Santa!"

"I am so proud of you, Allie." Mommy said, hugging us. "Would you believe it? Some children were too scared to sit on Santa's lap!"

"Not me," I told her.

Santa's beard wasn't weird after all. It was just my crazy imagination!

At first, I was afraid of Santa, but I'm so glad I gave him a chance. Now visiting him is my favorite thing to do at Christmas!'

Printed in the USA
CPSIA information can be obtained
at www.ICGtesting.com
CBHW042043051124
16958CB00013B/253